Little Yellow Pear Tomatoes

By Demian Elainé Yumei
Illustrated by Nicole Tamarin

*Inspired by the teachings of Thich Nhat Hanh
and written for my daughter, Brhiannon,
who really does love little yellow pear tomatoes.*

*Special thanks to Terri Cohlene;
as big a part of this little book
as the stars are in little tomatoes.*

~DEY

*For my driving force throughout this project
as well as in life,
my mother.*

~NT

Little Yellow Pear Tomatoes

By Demian Elainé Yumei
Illustrated by Nicole Tamarin

ILLUMINATION Arts

PUBLISHING COMPANY, INC.

Bellevue, Washington

I love little yellow pear tomatoes.

They are not red or round like
other tomatoes. They are yellow
and pear-shaped, and they
come out of our garden.

They are so small *and* they are SO big. Not because of their size, but because of what's inside!

A lot of *not-a-tomato* things are in these little yellow pear tomatoes.

Daddy plants them for me.
He tills the soil and puts up stakes
for them to lean against. Without him
they would not be in our garden.

My daddy is in these little
yellow pear tomatoes.

Mommy pulls the weeds. She makes room for
all the young plants to grow. Without her
the weeds would cover them up.

My mommy is in these little yellow pear tomatoes.

Ladybugs and earthworms live in our garden.

They keep away pests and dig tunnels in the ground.

Without ladybugs and earthworms,
the leaves on our plants would
get eaten and their roots
couldn't breathe.

Ladybugs and earthworms
are in these little yellow
pear tomatoes.

Clouds water our garden with rain. Lakes and rivers give their water to the sky to make into clouds. Without fresh water our plants could not live.

Clouds and lakes and rivers and sky are in these little yellow pear tomatoes.

The sun gives its energy to each leaf, making it
strong and green. The leaves turn this energy into
life for the whole plant. Without the sun,
our plants would wither and die.

The sun is in these little
yellow pear tomatoes.

The sun is a star, and everything needed
to make a planet is found in the hearts of stars.

Without them, there would be no earth or skies
or rivers. No daddies to till the rich,
dark soil. No tomato seeds!

Stars are in these little yellow pear tomatoes.

All these *not-a-tomato* things – my daddy,
my mommy, bugs and worms, clouds and sky, lakes
and rivers, the sun and stars – are parts of
the tomato you cannot see. Take away any one,
and the little yellow pear tomatoes
in my garden could not be.

With so much in them, you would
think these tomatoes would be HUGE! But they aren't.
I can carry four or five in my hand and pop
them into my mouth, one by one.

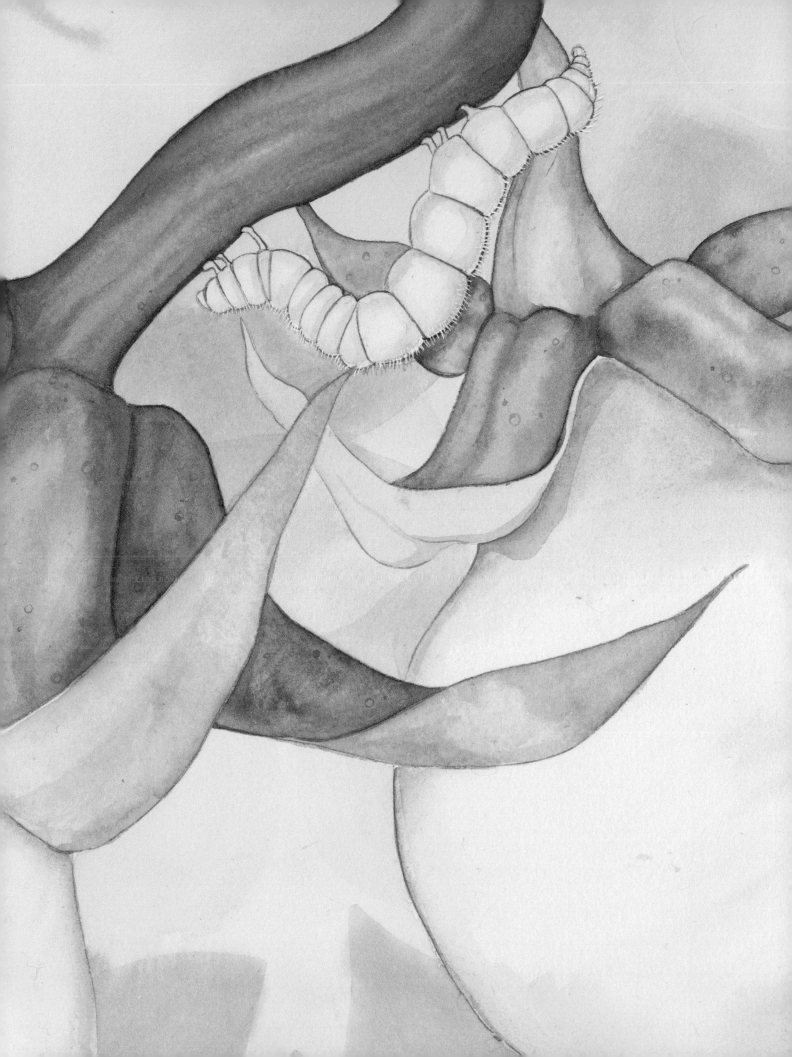

I am in these little yellow pear tomatoes, too,
because if I didn't love eating them
so much, my daddy wouldn't plant them!

Each little yellow pear tomato
has the entire earth and all of heaven
in it...just like me.

I love little yellow pear tomatoes!

PUBLISHING COMPANY, INC.
P.O. Box 1865, Bellevue, WA 98009
Tel: 425-644-7185 ❧ 888-210-8216 (orders only) ❧ Fax: 425-644-9274
liteinfo@illumin.com ❧ www.illumin.com

Library of Congress Cataloging-in-Publication Data

Yumei, Demian.
  Little yellow pear tomatoes / written by Demian Yumei ; illustrated by Nicole Tamarin.
     p. cm.
  Summary: A young girl describes all of the things that go into her favorite tomatoes,
from worms to stars, that make them so wonderful to eat.
  ISBN 0-9740190-2-X (hardcover)
  [1. Tomatoes--Fiction. 2. Gardening--Fiction.] I. Tamarin, Nicole, ill. II. Title.
  PZ7.Y8966Li 2005
  [E]--dc22

                              2004026711

Published in the United States of America

Printed in Singapore by Tien Wah Press
Book Designer: Molly Murrah, Murrah & Company, Kirkland, WA

Illumination Arts Publishing Company, Inc. is a member of Publisher's in Partnership—
replanting our nation's forests.

A portion of the profits from this book will be donated to The Children's Global Foundation, a non-profit organization dedicated to global peace and to helping homeless children worldwide.

This foundation was formed by Children's Global Village (CGV), an organization of leading architects, engineers, developers, builders, and media specialists working together to promote advancements in education and environmentally safe solutions to society's problems. CGV's goal is to develop spiritually-based cities of the future around the world. In addition to futuristic schools, homes, offices and business developments, each city will have a world-class theme park providing culturally diverse education and entertainment. For more information on CGV cities of the future, contact cgv@illumin.com.

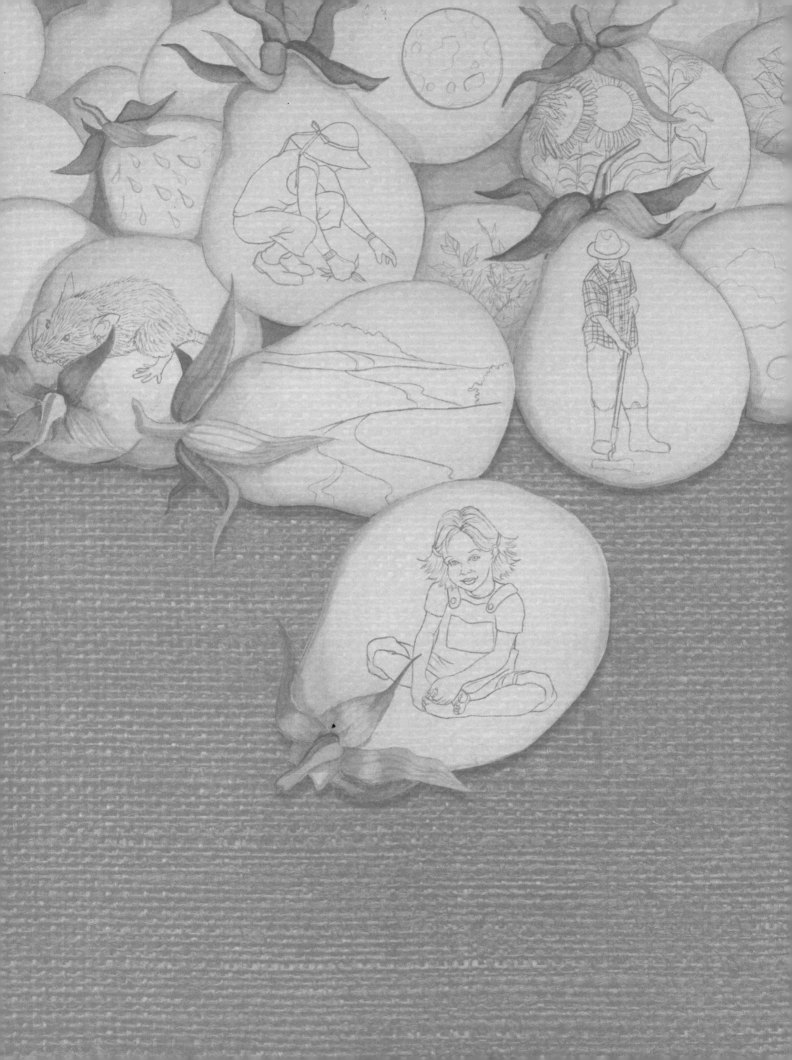